Joe's Big Adventure

pictures and story by

Dubravka Kolanovic

Penton
Kids Press

Joe was Max's hamster.
He lived in a small cage and
his life was rather dull.
He watched Max playing with
Digby, the dog. He longed
to play too.

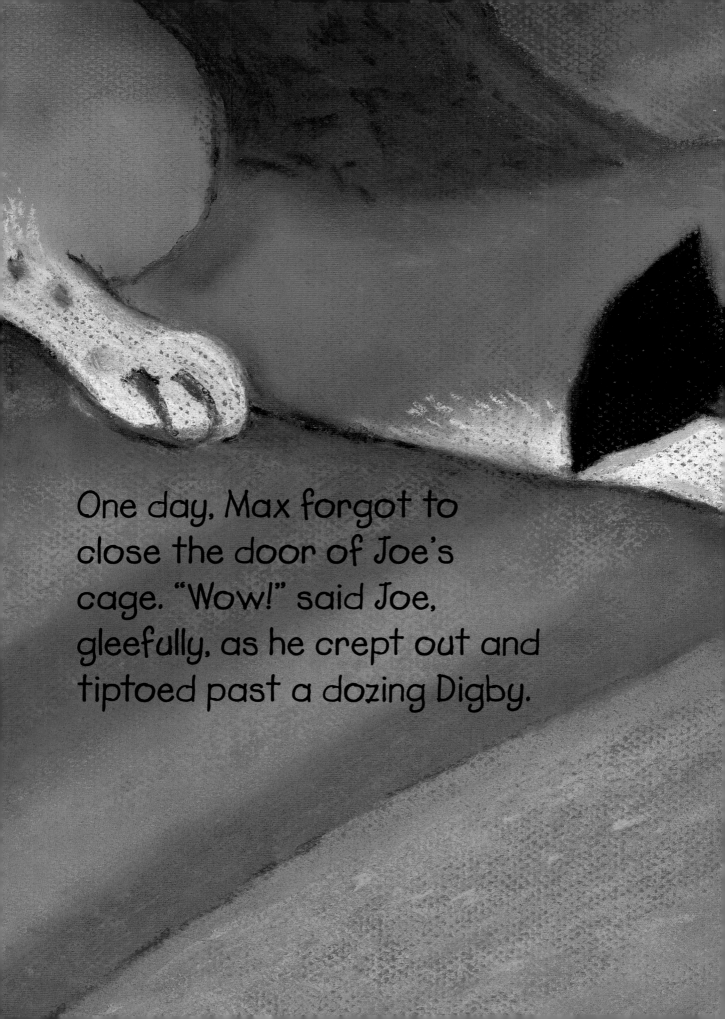

One day, Max forgot to close the door of Joe's cage. "Wow!" said Joe, gleefully, as he crept out and tiptoed past a dozing Digby.

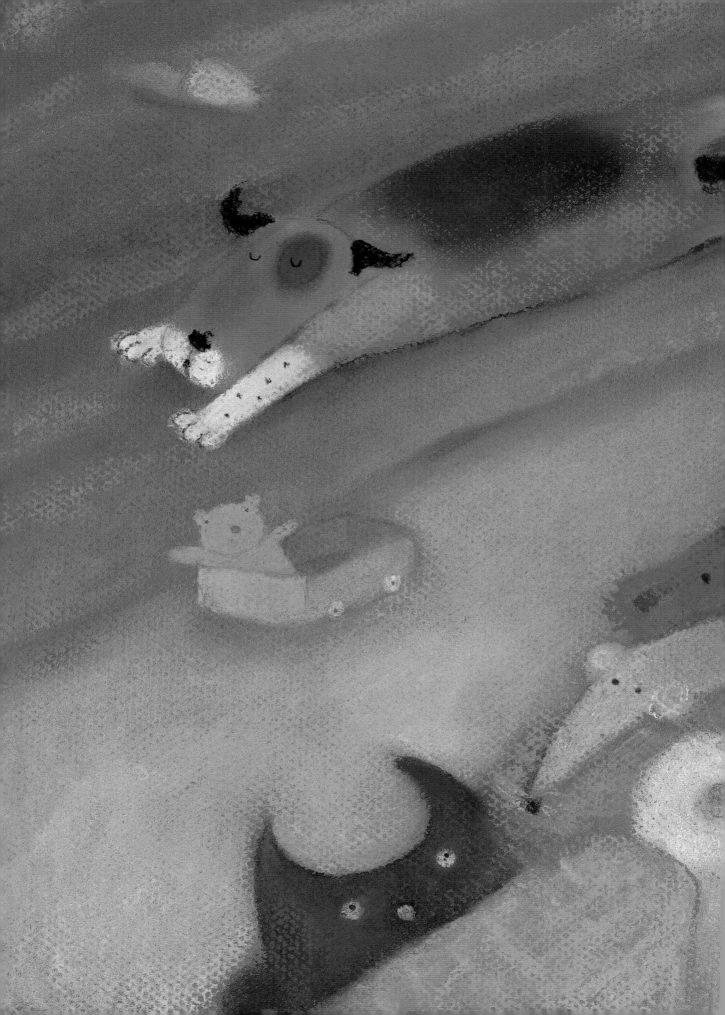

"What a mess!" thought Joe as he clambered over the toys on the carpet.

"Yum yum!" said Joe when he spotted a huge jar of strawberry jam and a very handy spoon. Max and Digby were too busy to notice.

"Oh, golly gumdrops!" said Joe when he discovered the jar of sweets. He ate one, then two, and then three, and then another, and another. When he'd lost count, he gave some to Digby.

"Oo er!" groaned Joe when his tummy was full. He and Digby stretched out for a snooze on the sofa.

"Yippee!" exclaimed Joe when he found some crumbs on the bookshelf. Digby said nothing.

"Tee hee!" chuckled Joe
when he spied the bath tub.
The water tickled his toes.
Digby didn't want a bath.

"Hello, handsome hamster!" chuckled Joe when he looked in the mirror. It was much bigger than the one in his cage. Digby sniffed the toothpaste.

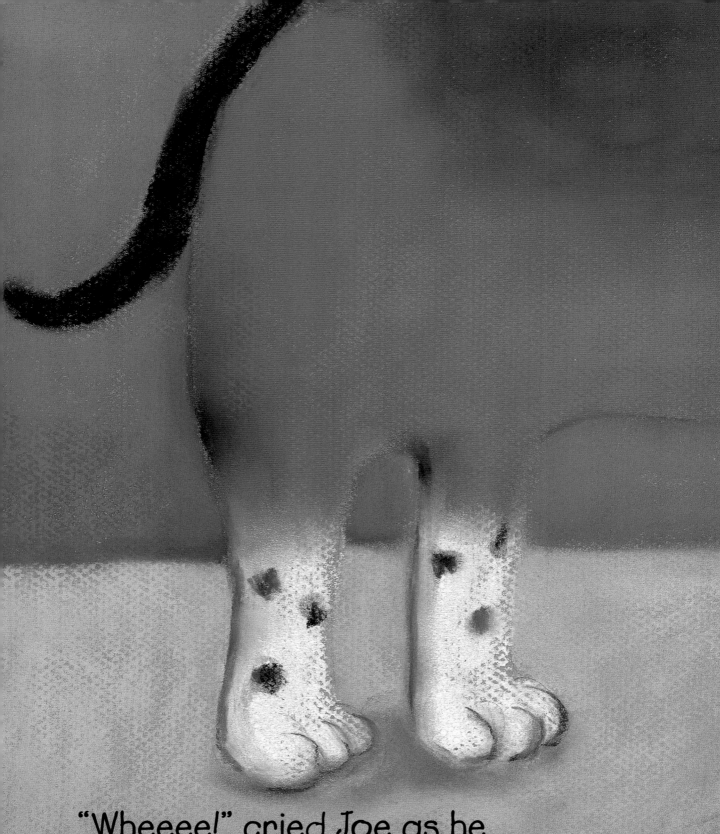

"Wheeee!" cried Joe as he whizzed down a high-heeled shoe on his tummy.

Digby chewed the other
shoe thoughtfully.

"Bleagh!" croaked
Joe as he took
a bite out of a
big fat leaf.
"That tastes
horrid!" Digby
wasn't sure this
was a good idea.

"Urgh! I feel sick!"
whispered Joe.
Digby looked
worried.

"Oh dear!"
said Max.
"I think we
need to
take you to
the vet."

"Boo hoo!" wailed Joe. It was very busy at the vet's and he was scared.

The vet was very kind. He poked Joe's tummy gently and declared, "Nothing wrong with you, young hamster. A bit of exercise is what you need!"

"Home, sweet home," squeaked Joe as he raced around his wheel. He felt much better. "I think I've had enough adventures for today!"

Digby just smiled.

Penton Kids Press™ is an imprint of Penton Overseas, Inc.
Carlsbad, CA
www.pentonoverseas.com

First published in North America 2005
1 3 5 7 9 10 8 6 4 2

Illustrations ©2004 Dubravka Kolanovic • English text and format ©2004 Tony Potter Publishing Ltd
Printed and bound in China • ISBN 1-59125-257-1